Deep Water

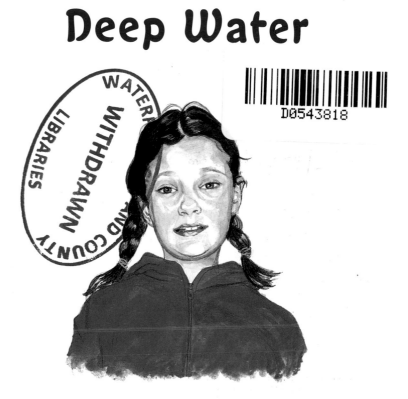

D0543818

Written by Judy Waite
Illustrated by Pamela Goodchild

Heinemann

For all of Class 2 at
Locks Heath Junior School, 1998-1999

Chapter 1

It was time to go home. There was
the usual scraping sound of chairs
being pushed back.

'Remember to work on your class
speeches for homework,' Miss
Walker called, as everyone started
talking and packing their school
bags. 'You can read them out first
thing in the morning.'

Jenny felt sick. Thinking about her speech made her tummy hurt. It felt as if she had a giant jellyfish squirming about inside her.

She hated having to read aloud in class. She was sure everyone got really bored listening to her.

Once, when Jenny was reading out her holiday diary, Lee West had even looked at his watch. Jenny noticed the flash of light as he held it up to get a better look.

Lee had a posh watch. It was a silver and blue one that you could wear for deep sea diving. Jenny had heard him laugh about it to someone once.

Still, even if his watch was fantastic to look at, he must have been really bored listening to Jenny THAT time.

Lee West was the sort of person who was never boring. He seemed so clever, and he always had loads of friends round him. He was always telling jokes, and giving the 'thumbs up' sign to people. He never did anything like that to Jenny. She sometimes wondered if he had ever even noticed her.

Jenny watched Lee walk ahead of her as they left school. He had a certain sort of walk. He had a certain sort of laugh. Jenny never quite knew what it was, but she wished she had it too. She was sure Lee never had giant jellyfish squirming round in his tummy. He probably had wonderful dolphins, all leaping about with a sleek, shining confidence.

Jenny sighed. Lee was just one of those people who was good at everything. She didn't think she was good at anything much – only swimming.

Mum took her for lessons every morning, before most people were even up.

Lee disappeared out of the school gate and into the alley. He was talking to an older girl from the next class up. They were laughing loudly, as if they had just heard the funniest joke in the world.

Jenny trailed along behind. As she walked, she stared down at the scuffed toes of her supermarket trainers. Lee had those designer sports trainers, of course. They were the sort you saw on the telly adverts. Mum had said there wasn't any point buying things like that. 'You grow too quickly,' she always grumbled. Mum seemed to think Jenny grew too quickly on purpose, just as an excuse to get new clothes.

If Jenny hadn't been staring at her trainers, she might have missed it. But as she turned the corner into the alley, she nearly trod on it. Lee's watch – the posh, deep sea diving one – was lying right in the middle of the path.

Jenny knew she should just pick it up and give it back to him, but she didn't want to have to run after him. Suppose she had to call out his name? Suppose she had to tap him on the back? Just the thought of it made the jellyfish in her tummy start squirming again.

The best thing to do would be to take the watch home. She could get to school early, after swimming, and hand it in to the office before Lee got there.

Jenny bent down quickly and picked up the watch. Then she pushed it into the pocket of her school bag, and ran home.

Chapter 2

'I am going to talk about swimming. Swimming is something that...,' Jenny's voice trailed away. Miss Walker had told them all to practise in front of the mirror. She said it would help – but it didn't seem to be working for Jenny. Her face looked as white as chalk. And her eyes were wide with panic.

If she looked like this tomorrow, the class would think she'd been taken over by aliens. They'd probably all make a run for the door.

She took a deep breath and started again. 'I am going to talk about swimming. Swimming is something that…'

Jenny scrunched up the notes she'd been reading from and threw them down on the dressing table. Swimming wasn't anything special. Anyone could do it. All you had to do was float round and kick your legs about. What was so brilliant about that?

Perhaps she could pretend to Miss Walker that she'd lost her voice. She stared at herself again, mouthing the words. She looked like a goldfish saying its prayers. Still, it was probably more interesting than her speech.

Jenny flopped down on to the bed. Her school bag was there. She hugged it as if it was a teddy bear, and she cried.

Long shadows crept into her room. Jenny heard the evening paper plop through the letter box. A smell of onions was coming up from the kitchen.

She sat up slowly. She had to be sensible. Mum would be calling her for dinner soon. Jenny didn't want Mum to know she'd been crying.

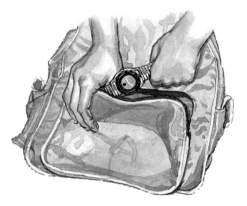

She unzipped the pocket of her school bag, searching for the neatly folded hankie Mum always tucked in there. Instead, her fingers touched the cold, silver strap of Lee's watch.

Jenny turned it over and over in her hand. The numbers round the edge of the face were the sort that glow in the dark. There was a button to press to show how deep you were diving. There was a tiny window that showed what the temperature was. Jenny let the watch lie against her wrist. She liked the silver against the pale white of her skin.

Almost without thinking, Jenny put it on.

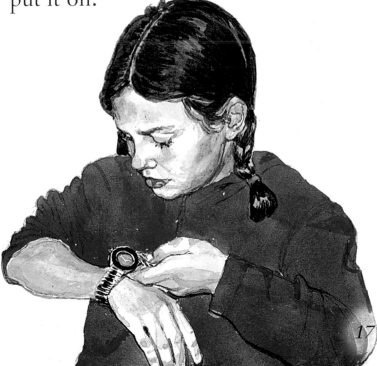

She was surprised it fitted so well.
It felt a bit heavy, but she didn't mind
the heaviness. It made her feel
important. Powerful.

She got up and walked over to the
mirror again. She still looked pale
and boring. Slowly, she pulled her
shoulders back and stood up
straighter. She tilted her chin slightly,
the way Lee sometimes did. It made
her face look different – stronger
somehow.

Her scrunched-up speech was still there, lying near her hairbrush. Jenny opened it out again.

Im going to talk about swimming
Swimming is something I started when
I was three years old.
very soon, my swimming teacher said

Jenny found that, after a moment, she wasn't even reading from the sheet.

Thoughts and ideas seemed to flow through her. 'I have been lucky. I've won lots of competitions. But when I'm in a race, I'm not really thinking about winning. I'm just loving the feeling of being in the water. It's as if I'm gliding through it, like a fish...'

As the words flooded out of her, Jenny giggled with excitement. She suddenly seemed to have a certain sort of laugh. She swung round and walked across the room. She suddenly seemed to have a certain sort of walk.

Turning back to the mirror, Jenny saw a flash of light from the watch in the glass. The flashes of silver seemed almost magical. So maybe that was it. Maybe Lee's watch really DID have something magic about it. Maybe that was his secret.

'Jenny, dinner time!' Mum called from downstairs. Jenny felt unhappy suddenly. What did she think she was doing? Even if Lee's watch did have a special power, it wasn't much use to her. She'd have to give it back tomorrow, anyway.

'Jenny!'

'Coming!' Jenny slowly unfastened the watch. Already, her face in the mirror seemed to be growing paler, growing more boring. By tomorrow morning she'd be right back where she'd started.

Unless...

She pushed the thought away. She couldn't do it. It would be wrong. She might get into trouble.

But then again, it wouldn't need to be for very long.

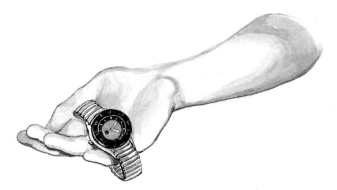

Chapter 3

The sun spilled in through the classroom window. It was a warm day, but Jenny was wearing her thick winter jumper. She felt hot and uncomfortable, but she needed its long sleeves to cover her wrist. She hoped no one would notice how nervous she looked.

'Now then,' Miss Walker smiled round at the class, 'I'm sure you've all got some lovely speeches prepared for me so – who's going to be very brave and go first?'

Nobody moved.

'Come on now. I can't wait to hear about all of your wonderful hobbies.'

Jenny's hand didn't shoot up. The watch's powers weren't that magical. But as she raised her arm slowly into the air, she kept her back straight and her chin up. 'I'll go first, Miss Walker.'

Miss Walker looked surprised. 'Are you quite sure?' she said.

'I just want to get it over with.' Jenny kept her hand up as she spoke, waving it round slightly, like she'd seen Lee West do.

'All right then. Would you...' Miss Walker never finished her sentence, because there was a shout from behind.

'She's stolen my watch!'

Jenny's hand, still stuck in the air, seemed to freeze. Something terrible had happened! The sleeve of her jumper had slipped back! The magical blue and silver watch shone and glittered on her wrist, like a thousand jewels. She slumped back in her chair. She looked down at the table. She knew that everyone was staring at her. The jellyfish in her tummy woke up.

'It went missing at school yesterday,' Lee said, angrily. 'I realised it when I got home. My dad's furious.'

'Jenny?' Miss Walker's voice was as sharp as a knife.

Jenny didn't answer. How could she possibly explain about the watch, and the magic, and the way it was going to help her? No one would understand. No one would believe her.

Miss Walker sighed. 'You'd better give Lee his watch, and then go and see the Headmaster. Perhaps he can get some sense out of you.'

Mr Atkins, the Headmaster, frowned at Jenny. His eyes looked very fierce beneath his huge, hairy eyebrows. 'You had better tell me why you're here.'

'I-I know I shouldn't have done it,' Jenny stuttered.

'Done what?' asked Mr Atkins.

Jenny felt sick. She wondered what Mr Atkins would do. He'd probably tell her mum. He'd probably tell Lee West's dad. He might even call the police.

At the thought of the police, the jellyfish in her tummy did three giant somersaults. 'I...'

At that moment there was a knock on the door.

Lee West peered round.

'Not now, Lee.' Mr Atkins frowned again. 'Can't you see I'm busy?'

'But it's about Jenny, sir. It's important,' said Lee.

One hairy eyebrow raised itself slowly. 'What is it you want to say?'

Lee didn't look at Mr Atkins. Instead, he turned to Jenny. 'I'm really sorry. I've only just remembered – you couldn't have stolen my watch. My cousin Meg was teasing me about it, on the way home from school yesterday.'

'I found it,' Jenny blurted out. 'I was going to give it back this morning, but I - I wanted to wear it for a little while, just until the speeches were over.'

Now it was Lee's turn to frown. 'But why?'

'I wanted to wear it while I was giving my speech. I'm sorry. I know it sounds stupid.'

Lee still looked puzzled. 'It's a smart watch — it looks good and everything, but it's not THAT great.'

Mr Atkins said suddenly, 'I don't know what's going on, but you seem to have sorted it out between yourselves. You'd better get back to class.'

Lee chatted as they walked together, back down the corridor. 'Miss Walker made the others do some maths while she talked to me about the watch. It was only then that I remembered when I was last wearing it.'

But Jenny wasn't listening. She was just glad that she wasn't in trouble after all.

'So that means you're lucky, doesn't it?' Lee went on.

Jenny looked at him, suddenly realising he had asked her a question. 'Why?' she asked.

'Well, we haven't started the speeches yet. Miss Walker was saving them until you got back. You'll still be able to go first, like you wanted.'

Chapter 4

The whole class was sitting on the carpet in a half circle, in front of Miss Walker.

'Okay, Jenny,' said Miss Walker, giving her a bright smile, 'we're all ready for you.'

Jenny walked slowly towards the front of the class. She couldn't think properly. All round her, a sea of faces was watching. Jenny felt frightened, as if she was drowning in her own terror.

Suddenly, she saw a flash of something bright. Lee West, at the back of the class, was rolling up his sleeves. Jenny saw the silvery flash of the watch on his wrist. It still looked special. It still looked magical. Jenny lifted her head slowly, and looked straight at Lee. He was sitting very straight. His chin was turned upwards slightly. As soon as Lee realised that Jenny was watching him, he gave her a quick 'thumbs up' sign.

Jenny pulled back her shoulders. She lifted her head high. She took a deep breath, like someone who was about to dive into deep, deep water. 'I am going to talk about swimming. Swimming is something that...'

It was ten minutes later when Miss Walker stopped her. 'That was a fantastic speech, Jenny. How wonderful to have a talent like that. Now, who's going to go next...?'

At break time, Lee found Jenny in the playground. 'Your speech was great. It must be really hard work, getting up so early in the morning and everything,' he said.

'I'm just used to it. I don't think about it,' said Jenny.

'Still, you're lucky. I wish I could do something like that. I can't even swim.'

Jenny looked amazed. 'But – the watch. I thought you must be able to swim because your watch is the kind you can wear underwater.'

'Only in my dreams. My dad gets them cheap. He's got a market stall, and sells all sorts of stuff – trainers, sports gear, jewellery.'

Lee laughed. 'It's not really a very good watch. It doesn't keep time very well.' He showed Jenny the watch. 'I set it after I got it back from you, but it's already ten minutes slow.'

Jenny stared at him for a moment. She didn't know what to think, or say.

'Here.' Lee undid the strap. 'You can wear it if you like. Borrow it for the day.'

Jenny looked down at the watch. The bright sun was dancing all over the silver making it look more sparkly than ever. Suddenly, she shook her head. 'Thanks, but I'd better not. I might lose it or something.' She smiled, remembering how everyone had crowded round her in class earlier.

They had asked her lots of questions about swimming. 'I don't think I really need the watch anymore,' added Jenny.

Lee put the watch back on. 'Let me know if you change your mind.' He gave her a quick grin, and ran off.

Jenny watched him go. She didn't move, but inside her tummy she felt something move. It was as if a wonderful dolphin had just gone leaping through her.

About the author

Judy Waite

I didn't start writing until I had my own children. When they were little, I wrote stories for comics. Now I have more time to write books.

As well as being an author, I also work in a junior school. This is great because I can sometimes pick up ideas from the things children in my class say and do.

The idea for *Deep Water* came after a girl in my class, called Louise, won the school speech competition. She spoke clearly and with confidence and I began thinking what it would be like to be the opposite of Louise – scared and worried. And that is how this story began!

About the illustrator
Pamela Goodchild

I started drawing 'ladies'
on my great aunt's knee
when I was three, and
when I was ten, my grandfather made
me my own easel.

I use water colours for my pictures
and oil paint for larger portraits. I love
to paint children, and often use my own
children as models. For Jenny in this
book my daughter, Roseanna, was my
model.

I work on my kitchen table, and
Paddy, my dog, often sits at my feet
while I'm working. This is fine, until he
moves and jogs the table! I've used him
in my pictures too!